UNCLE WILLIE
AND THE SOUP KITCHEN
DyANNE DiSALVO-RYAN

A Mulberry Paperback Book   New York

This book is lovingly dedicated to the friends and family
of Mr. William Hearne—the real Uncle Willie

The art is a diazo print done with watercolors and colored pencils
and reproduced in full color.

The text type is 13 point ITC Cushing Book.

The Library of Congress has cataloged the Morrow Junior Books
edition of *Uncle Willie and the Soup Kitchen* as follows:
DiSalvo-Ryan, DyAnne.
Uncle Willie and the soup kitchen / DyAnne DiSalvo-Ryan.
p. cm.
Summary: A boy spends the day with Uncle Willie in the soup
kitchen where he works preparing and serving food for the hungry.
ISBN 0-688-09165-2.—ISBN 0-688-09166-0 (lib. bdg.)
[1. Soup kitchens—Fiction.] I. Title.
PZ7.D6224Un 1991 90-6375 CIP AC
[E]—dc20

5 7 9 10 8 6 4
First Mulberry Edition, 1997
ISBN 0-688-15285-6

About Soup Kitchens

Each day in cities all across the country, volunteers and paid workers prepare meals to feed millions of hungry men, women, and children who come to eat at local soup kitchens. Religious organizations, neighborhood stores, food banks, money donations, and government subsidies support these efforts to provide hot meals to the poor.

Nationally, about one out of every eight people is poor. Many of them are children. It isn't necessary for patrons of soup kitchens to be unemployed or homeless. Sometimes working people do not make enough money to provide basic needs and comforts for themselves or their families. Many elderly people and others living on small fixed incomes depend on soup kitchens for their main meal.

Bread for the World, Results, Second Harvest, the National Network of Food Banks, and the Food Hunger Hotline are a few of the hundreds of local and national organizations that exist to meet the growing needs of the hungry in our neighborhoods today.

CHARLES "PUNCH" WOODS
Executive Director, Community Food Bank, Inc.
South Tucson, Arizona

"Talk to me," says Uncle Willie when he picks me up from school. I go down the steps like a house on fire. "Race you to the corner," I yell without stopping. Uncle Willie pretends to wobble on his string-bean legs. He makes me laugh so hard that he gets to the corner before I do. While Mom's at work, Uncle Willie's job is to keep an eye on me. This is fine with me and it's just fine with Uncle Willie. But during the day while I'm at school, my Uncle Willie has another job. He works at the soup kitchen.

"We fed a lot of people today," says Uncle Willie. "Spaghetti and meatballs. Good thing the bakery truck stopped by to give us extra bread." Uncle Willie checks his pocket and sprinkles crumbs onto the sidewalk.

I check my pocket, too, and pull out my paper telescope. "Why do you work there, anyway?" I ask, eyeballing Uncle Willie. "It's important," Uncle Willie tells me. "Sometimes people need help."

Way up the block, I hear the Can Man's clangity cart, piled high with empty cans he finds in our neighborhood. My mom says he cashes them in for money at the supermarket. Whenever I see the Can Man, he is pushing his shopping cart in the street. Today he's on the sidewalk, though, moving his clangity cart right toward us.

"Let's go," I whisper to Uncle Willie. But I think he doesn't hear me. "How's business, Frank?" Uncle Willie hollers. "One more block and I'm done for the day," the Can Man hollers back. Uncle Willie picks up an empty can and tosses it into the cart. "Two points for the basket," the Can Man says. Then he hunches back over his cart to give it one long push.

I listen to the sound of those rattly wheels, *clangity bump, clangity bump*, until they are far, far away. "Since when do you know that can man?" I ask Uncle Willie. "Since Frank came to eat at the soup kitchen," he says. "But why doesn't Frank eat in his own house?" I ask. "Doesn't he have a place to live?" Uncle Willie takes my hand and rocks it high and low. "I never asked Frank where he lived," says Uncle Willie. "In the soup kitchen, you only have to be hungry."

When Mom walks me to school the next morning, I see a woman sleeping on the park bench. "She looks lonely," I say. I feel kind of sad when I see her. Mom says there're a lot of lonely people these days. "That's why I'm proud of Uncle Willie. He's doing something to help."

"But I wonder what it's like to work inside a soup kitchen. I mean, Uncle Willie goes there almost every single day and I've never even gone with him once." Mom hands me my milk money and scoots me up the front steps. "Why don't you ask Uncle Willie to take you next Monday?" says Mom. "Remember, you have a day off from school."

"All set?" asks Uncle Willie, bright and early Monday morning. "All set," I say. I check my pocket and pull out my telescope. Uncle Willie grabs his cap and stuffs his pockets with bread. Mom kisses me good-bye and tells us both to keep out of trouble.

The soup kitchen is not too far from where I live, but it feels like a very long way. We pass my school. We pass the supermarket, the drugstore, the bakery, and the laundry. When we get to Mr. Anthony's Meat Market, I am dragging my feet. "Let's stop and see if Mr. Anthony has anything for us today," says Uncle Willie.

Mr. Anthony's door has a little bell on top that rings whenever it opens. "Hello, already," Uncle Willie hollers. "Hello, yourself," Mr. Anthony says. "Have I got something special for you!" When Mr. Anthony comes out from the back, he hands Uncle Willie a lumpy brown bag. He gives me a brown bag, too. "Chicken for the soup," Mr. Anthony tells us. "Food for a feast," says Uncle Willie. The little bell rings again when the door closes, and I wave good-bye through the big front window.

When we turn the corner, Uncle Willie points to a small brick building. It looks old and kind of run-down from the outside. "Here we are," he says. A woman opens the big white door. "Good morning, Shanta," says Uncle Willie. "A very good morning," says Shanta, smiling. "You brought us a helper today." I shake Shanta's hand and follow Uncle Willie inside.

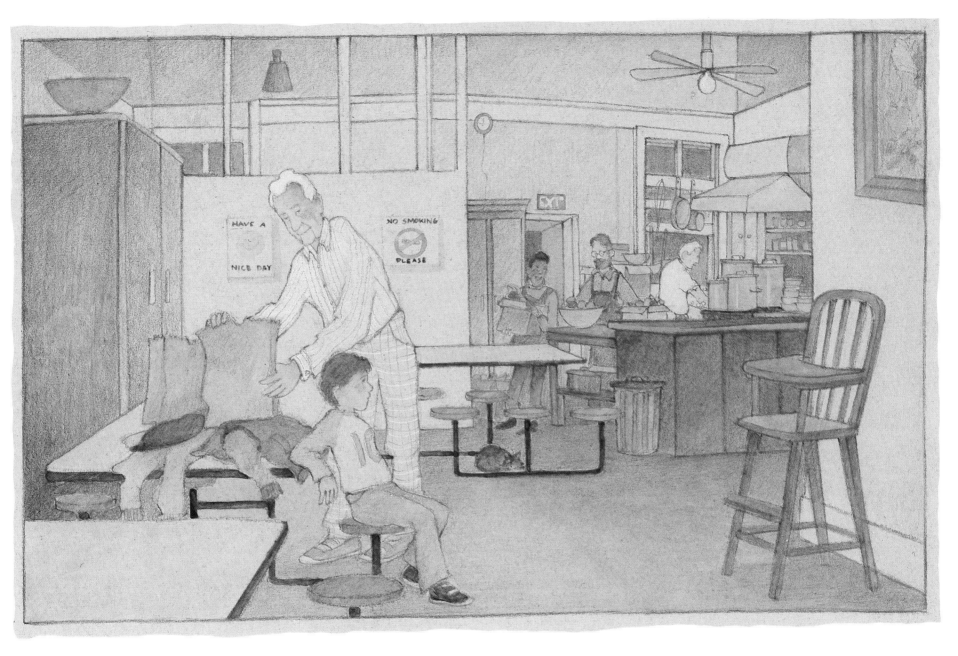

The soup kitchen is small and bright. The four huge soup pots steaming on the stove make the whole place smell delicious. There are posters on the wall that say: HAVE A NICE DAY and NO SMOKING PLEASE. "Look!" I say. "Lunchroom tables just like my school. But what's that high chair doing there?" Uncle Willie takes my bag and puts it down on the table. "Little children come here, too."

"Now let me introduce you all around," says Uncle Willie. First I meet a cat. "This is Underfoot," Uncle Willie tells me. "Underfoot works the night shift down in the basement. And over there is Brother Mike." Brother Mike opens the lumpy bags from Mr. Anthony's store and turns them upside down. "Chickens," he says, looking over at us. "That's great! Thanks for picking them up."

A man at the double sink is washing a big silver bowl. "And this is George," Uncle Willie says. "If it wasn't for George, we'd all be in hot water." Uncle Willie ties an apron on and helps me tie one, too. "Now let's get to work, already."

I watch Uncle Willie cut the celery short and skinny and split the tomatoes in fours. He chops the potatoes and parsley and onions and tosses some into each soup pot. He smiles at me and jiggles a carrot. "Poifect." Uncle Willie hoots and finishes off the string beans.

"Will you help me sort the fruits and vegetables?" Shanta asks. "The market gave us so much fruit that we can make a salad today." I separate the fruit and put it in the sink to wash. While Shanta slices, I mix the fruit inside the big silver bowl with a wooden spoon.

Everything comes extra big around here. George walks over from the sink and opens a really big can of peanuts. He says he wouldn't mind one bit if he had some extra help. I put one big bowl of peanuts, one big plate of sliced cheese, one big dish of butter, and two big baskets of bread on every lunchroom table.

"Mmmmm, I'm hungry," I say when Brother Mike gives every pot just one more stir. "Break time," he says. "Help yourself to a bowl of soup." "Sit down, already," Uncle Willie tells me. "And make yourself uncomfortable." I pour a little bit of my soup into a cup for Underfoot. "Chicken and vegetable soup," I say. "My favorite." I look around at all the empty chairs. "But what if there's not enough soup?" I ask.

Uncle Willie waves his hands. "It's just like magic," he tells me. "There's always a little bit more." He pulls something out of his pocket. "This little clicker will count how many people come here today, so then we can make enough food for tomorrow."

When I'm finished eating, I peek outside and see a long line of people from the soup kitchen door to the corner. "I used to be out there on those lines," says George. "But now I'm in here helping."

I stare out the window and reach for Uncle Willie. "Are all those people homeless?" I whisper. "Is George homeless, too?" Uncle Willie leans a little closer and says, "George rents a room in a building nearby. But some of the people have no place to live. If they're here, they're hungry, and we're here to fill up the bowls."

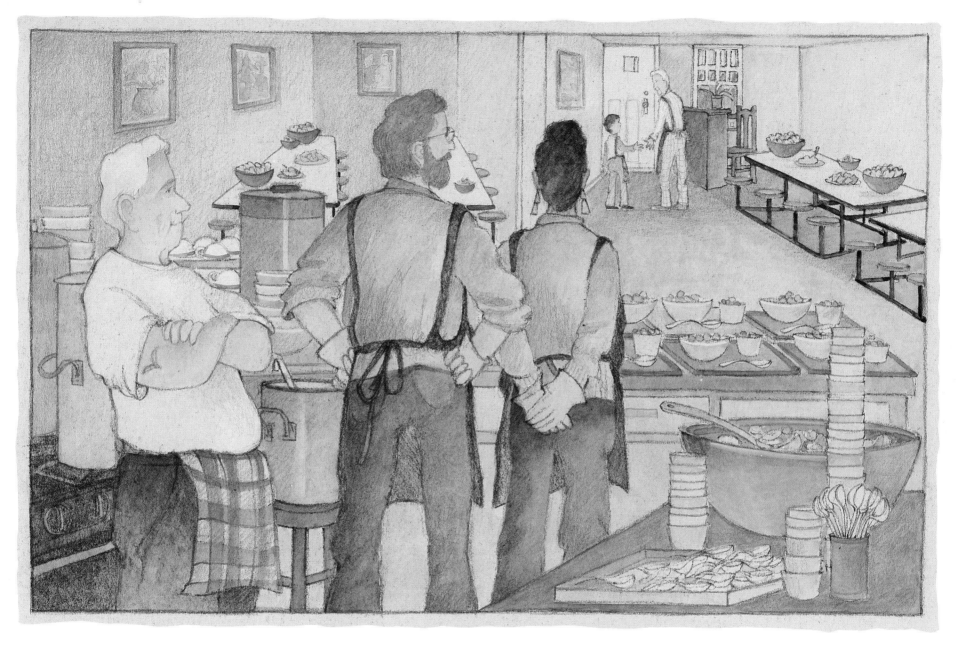

Brother Mike ladles the steaming soup into the bowls and places one on every tray. Shanta dishes out the fruit cups and puts them next to the bowls. When the first trays are ready with soup and fruit, Uncle Willie yells out, "Lunchtime!"

We let the big white door swing open and the first few people rush in at once. "The soup is nice and hot right from the pot," hollers Uncle Willie. He says hello to just about everybody who comes in. "And how are you, Double Jim?" asks Uncle Willie. Double Jim points to his belly and laughs. "I'm twice as hungry and two times as big," he says.

There are so many people pushing in at once that I can't see inside anymore. Some of the guests try to shake my hand, but I stand stiffly against the door. "He's got a day off from school," announces Uncle Willie, keeping his hand on my shoulder. "So he came by to see where I work." "There's Frank, the Can Man," I whisper. "Hello there, Frank," says Uncle Willie, showing him the boxes of fruits and vegetables. "Help yourself. We have extra today."

In no time, the soup kitchen is full. Shanta fills up the fruit cups one after the other while Brother Mike fills up the bowls. All of a sudden, it sounds to me as if everyone's talking at once. People go up to the counter and say, "This soup is great. Can I have seconds?" "You gave her more chicken than you gave me." "But I was in line first." "We need more bread on our table, please." "We want more butter on ours." "More cheese on ours."

I watch the guests go in and out—first hungry, then full; first hungry, then full. "Come on in," calls Uncle Willie. George is walking back and forth. He picks up the dirty dishes from the counter and carries them back to the sink. I can hear the soup spoons going *clink, clink, clink*.

A woman shuffles by and stuffs her pockets with bananas. She looks a little bit like the woman I saw sleeping on the park bench. I hope so. I hope she comes to eat at the soup kitchen. It's not so lonely here.

Before I know it, the line outside the soup kitchen is gone and so is all the fruit inside Shanta's silver bowl. A few of the guests stay to help us all clean up. I hold the dustpan steady while Double Jim sweeps a pile for me to scoop.

When Uncle Willie and I are ready to leave, we shake hands with all the helpers. Brother Mike pushes open the big front door. "Come again anytime," he says. "We can always use the extra help."

"Thanks again for the soup," I holler to everyone else in the back. "Underfoot liked it, too."

On the way home, Uncle Willie shows me the counter. "We fed one hundred and twenty-one people today," he tells me. "That's a lot of citizens."

I pull my paper telescope out of my pocket and eyeball Uncle Willie. Uncle Willie looks like one big smile. Laughing, he picks up an empty can and hands it to me. I take the can and head for the trash. I turn. I fake. I jump. I shoot. "Talk to me," says Uncle Willie, and he hoots as I score two more points for the basket.